Table of Contents

Fly Away Little Bird

Kate looked up at the sky from her position on the roof of her playhouse. She loved staring into the sky at this time of day; the clouds were forming pictures that Kate could see in her mind. The sunshine warmed her skin and made Kate feel happy inside and out.

She heard a noise and turned to find Emily, Kate's babysitter, sitting on a chair close to the pool. Summer days were always Kate's favorite days. Her older brother was spending the day with his friends, and Emily had just put her younger brother down for a nap. The best time, in Kate's mind, was the time she and Emily spent together. She never really got the chance to spend as much time with her babysitter as her brothers did. Kate always seemed to have activities after school which meant she didn't see Emily that much.

"Hey, Kate," Emily called. Kate looked away from the blue sky above and toward Emily.

"Yeah?" she responded.

"Be careful up there, okay? I don't want you to fall," Emily said, and Kate nodded her head in answer. Satisfied with her response, Emily went back to reading her book.

Kate made herself

comfortable on the playhouse roof once again. She loved to climb on to the top of things and see the world from up high. Laying back against the roof, Kate tried to find as many pictures in the clouds as she could. While she did that, something in the nearby tree caught her eye. It looked like a bird's nest. Kate smiled at that thought, as she adored animals.

"Emily, look! There's a bird's nest in the tree!" Kate pointed to it and called out to her babysitter, excitedly.

"Really? That's awesome, Kate," Emily responded as she stretched her body out underneath the summer sun.

The little girl kept her eye on the bird's nest, wondering what it would be like to be a bird. *I wonder if I would be able to fly and explore the world like they do?*

As this thought ran through Kate's mind, she saw something fall from the nest. Curious, Kate sat up and stared at the ground, searching for the object that came out of nowhere. Not seeing it at first, she climbed down from her rooftop and searched the ground properly.

Kate wasn't too sure what she was looking for, as she didn't clearly see what fell. But halfway through her search, Kate spotted a broken egg lying just beneath the tree. *This is probably what I was searching for!* she thought to herself, happy with the discovery she had made.

Stepping closer to the shell, Kate's sneakers became dirty from the mud on the ground. It had rained that morning which made everything slightly wet. As she bent down, Kate thought about what she might find in the egg. There had been nothing in the eggshells she'd found before, but this one was different. This eggshell had just fallen out of the nest.

Kate moved closer to it when she saw something move inside. Curiosity grabbing her, she used her small finger to pull away the remains of the eggshell and what Kate found delighted her. Although, it also made her nervous.

"Emily! Come quick!" Kate shouted. Emily heard Kate's shout and slowly made her way to where the little girl was crouching.

"Quickly, Emily! Come quick!" Kate shouted again and saw that Emily was now walking faster. Soon, her pretty babysitter was crouching down next to her.

"What's wrong, Kate?" Emily questioned.

"Look!" Kate pointed toward the eggshell and the little creature inside.

"Where did that come from?" Emily asked, as she was curious about the broken egg and the creature inside it as well.

"It fell out of the tree. I think it's a baby bird," Kate replied and moved closer to the broken egg.

"Careful, Kate," Emily warned. "You don't want to hurt it."

"I'll be careful. I promise, Emily." As the little girl got closer to the shell, she saw that there really was a bird, but it was struggling to get up.

"Emily, it is a baby bird! It looks very sad. What should we do?"

Emily peered closer at it and replied in a whisper, "I don't know, Kate. What do you think we should do?"

Kate thought about it for a moment while the two girls stared at the bird. They were both trying to figure out how to help it when Kate suddenly thought of a conversation she had with her parents a few days earlier.

They told her that it's very important to always be kind to everyone and everything because you never know what they are going through. Or what their life is like. Her mom said it's a very important part in being a good person.

"Hey, Emily?" Kate called and tapped her babysitter on the shoulder.

"Yeah?" Again, Emily whispered, which made Kate lower her voice as well.

"The other day, my parents were talking to me about kindness and they said the best person I can be is one that is kind to everyone and everything. No matter who they are or where they are in life."

"That's a very important lesson to learn, Kay." Using Kate's nickname made her smile as she looked back at the baby bird.

"I think we should take care of it and make the baby bird feel better. What do you think?"

Mmm, Emily thought. "That's a good idea, Kate. But I think we should take it to the vet so that it can get the proper treatment that it needs. What do you think about that idea?"

4

"Good idea, Emily! Let's go find something to put it in."

"Why don't you stay here and make sure that nothing happen to it. I'll find something safe to put the baby bird in." Kate nodded her head as Emily walked toward the house.

While she was waiting for Emily, Kate thought about all the things that a little bird could do. *Would it be able to eat by itself? Would it be able to fly?* Kate slowly moved forward and gently picked up the baby bird. Just then, Emily came running back with a soft blanket in a tupperware container. She motioned for Kate to place the bird into it. After asking their neighbor to watch Kate's little brother, they made their way to the vet.

It wasn't a long drive as they were around the corner from the clinic, but Emily had buckled Kate in, placing the baby bird on her lap. Kate was worried about it during the drive and really hoped that the vet could help.

They arrived at the veterinary clinic and Emily spoke with the lady at the counter. She asked to see the vet while Kate sat down on a chair, whispering calming words to the baby bird.

"Don't worry, baby bird. You're going to be okay. We're getting you help and the vet is going to make you feel better." Emily had just sat down next to her when the vet called them in.

"So, what do we have here?" The vet said. She was an older woman with kind eyes and sparkling blonde hair.

Kate handed the tupperware to the woman. "I think it fell out of its nest. I was watching the tree when something fell out of it. We didn't know what to do, so we thought we'd bring it here."

"Well, that was an excellent thing to do, thank you. Let me have a look at it for you."

Kate was still worried while the kind woman looked at the bird. Emily placed her arm over her shoulder and Kate hugged her side, seeking comfort as she was scared for the bird.

"Okay," the vet started. "We might have to keep this little boy here for a couple of days, just to make sure that he is okay. After that, you can take him home and care for him for a few more weeks. Then you will have to let him go. Is that okay with you?"

Kate stared between the woman and the bird before finally looking up at Emily for reassurance, "Emily, what do you think we should do?"

Her babysitter hugged the little girl tighter and said, "I think that is a good idea. We'll be back in a couple of days, okay?"

Kate agreed, and they went home after saying goodbye to the baby bird. That night, Kate told her parents about what happened and they were proud of her for doing the right thing. She later went to sleep thinking about the bird and hoping that he was okay.

A few days later, Kate and Emily returned to the vet's office and were surprised when they saw the bird.

"Wow! He looks so much better," Kate said. She looked at the vet in awe as she handed Kate the bird.

"He sure does," the kind lady said with a smile on her face. She explained to them what had to be done to care for him and when they would have to let him go. They left the veterinary clinic and with the help of Emily, Kate cared for the bird as best as she could. He had grown so much in the few weeks that she had him, and it was finally time to set him free.

As her family gathered around her, Kate could feel sadness

creeping in, but she knew this was the best thing for the little bird. Her parents, brothers, and babysitter were all with her as she prepared to set it out on its own journey. Emily could tell that Kate was sad, so she came up to her and placed a comforting hand on Kate's shoulder. With a deep breath in, Kate finally let the bird go and he flew into his new life.

"I am so proud of you, Kay," Emily said. Her parents gave Kate a big hug as well.

"Kate," her mom said. "We are so proud of the beautiful girl you are becoming. What you did for that little bird was the best thing for it and it showed how much of a kind heart you have." Her dad agreed while adding that they loved her very much.

"I miss him already, but I know what I want to be when I grow up!"

"What is that?" her father asked. Everyone looked at her curiously as she thought about the past weeks and everything that happened.

"I want to be a vet like that kind lady and help animals as much as I can," Kate said with a big smile on her face.

Her parents and Emily thought it was a great idea while her brothers got excited about playing with the animals she would care for. As a family, they left the site where they released the baby bird and went to enjoy a wonderful meal together after a kind deed.

Let your dreams come true

Magic Land

The wind blew Ashley's dress as she made her way to the flower bud that her family called home. *Being a fairy is really fun when you can fly wherever you want to go*, Ashley thought to herself as she flew home.

Landing softly at the petal entrance, Ashley slowly made her way inside. She looked down at the dress she was wearing and thought about how much she loved it. Each fairy was special as everyone had a unique color given to them—Ashley's was yellow. She couldn't have been happier, as it was her favorite color. Most of the children at the fairy school didn't understand why she liked yellow instead of the colors that the other girls liked.

Ashley liked pink and purple too, but her absolute favorite would always be sunshine yellow. The best thing in her mind was that her fairy wings matched the color she got. Ashley looked back at her dark yellow wings and thought about how they looked like the sunflowers she

loved to play around in.

She didn't have many friends at school, but she had a best friend in a little dust bunny that Ashley found one day while playing in the sunflower fields. There were many things that Ashley liked about Magic Land. From the mystical animals to the little creatures she found, there were so many fascinating things in this magical nature.

Ashley found her dust bunny waiting for her on the bed that her father had made for her. Both her parents were builder fairies and loved to make things with their hands. For the rest of the afternoon, Ashley played with her dust bunny while waiting for her parents to come home. She eventually heard them arrive and flew out to greet them.

"Hey Ashley bear, how was school today?" Her father asked as she gave her mom a big hug. Her father called her over for a hug as well before sitting down at the wooden table.

"It was okay. Nothing special happened," she replied. Her mom began preparing Ashley's favorite dinner of pollen and dew while they sat around the table and talked about their day.

"Did you make any new friends, sweetie?" her mom asked. Ashley looked down at her tiny hands and shook her head.

"I don't know what's wrong with me, Mom. No one wants to be friends with me," she said sadly. Her mother stopped cooking and came to sit next to her. Both parents took one of Ashley's hands in their own and spoke reassuring words to her.

"Ashley, honey," her dad began. "You are beautiful, amazing, and strong. We are so proud and happy of the little fairy that you are. Don't be afraid to let someone else see how wonderful you are,

okay?"

The little yellow fairy felt tears come to her eyes as her mom pulled her into a tight embrace.

"Sweetie, you will make an amazing friend soon enough and when you do, the two of you will be the best of friends. I'm sure of it."

Ashley wiped her tears and gave her dust bunny a hug as he came out of her bedroom.

"Look at that!" Her father pointed to the dust bunny. "Even your dust bunny knows that you will make a friend soon. And this friend will be your best friend, honey. I know it's hard sometimes,

but being yourself is always better than trying to change who you are in order to make friends. If that is what you do, then those friends aren't really your friends."

"Your father's right, sweetie. Your genuine friends will love you for who you are and they will know that you are special because you don't pretend to be anyone else," her mom added.

Ashley understood what they were saying, as they have told her this for most of her 12 years of fairy life. She just hoped that she would make a best friend soon so that they could play together. They could also play with her dust bunny and have the most fun.

That night, Ashley and her parents had a delicious meal before saying goodnight and sleeping in a flower bud beneath the stars.

***

Ashley woke up the next morning thinking about what her parents had told her the night before. She really wanted to make friends, but Ashley was too scared to speak to any of the fairies at school. Speaking of school, she quickly flew down the familiar path that she took every morning and afternoon. Nothing seemed to have changed this particular morning until something flew into Ashley.

Startled, she stopped her flight and turned to see what had hit her. It wasn't something but rather, someone. Ashley recognized the purple fairy from one of her classes at school.

"Hey!" the purple fairy spoke with a small smile on her face. Ashley was confused, thinking that she must be speaking to someone behind her. She looked behind her and saw no one else was around. *Is the purple fairy talking to me?* she wondered.

"Hi." Ashley quietly answered. She didn't know what to do,

so she just flew around in the same spot and stared at the pretty fairy.

"You're Ashley, right?" she asked as she flew to meet Ashley's height.

"Yeah. I'm sorry, I don't know your name but I recognize you from school." Ashley replied with a bit of embarrassment.

"Oh! Don't worry," the purple fairy laughed, "My name's Brenna."

"That's such a pretty name! And I like your color, Brenna." Ashley said in response. She was feeling shy, as she hadn't spoken to any of the other fairies in a long time.

"Thank you, Ashley. I like your color too! Actually, I've been wanting to talk to you for a while!" Brenna said excitedly. Ashley still didn't understand what was happening. No one had come up to her before, let alone say that they wanted to speak with her.

"Oh, is there something that you need?" Ashley's heart felt sad as she hoped that the purple fairy wanted to be friends.

"Yeah, if you can help me?" Brenna didn't know that Ashley was about to cry when she heard those words. She just nodded her head for Brenna to continue.

"I was wondering if you would like to be my friend?" Her question made Ashley look up in surprise.

"Really? You want to be my friend?" she questioned. Ashley wasn't sure if she was hearing properly. Maybe she was dreaming?

"Yeah, of course! I always see you around, especially playing in the sunflowers. And you look like you have a lot of fun, so I thought we could do that together. What do you say?" Brenna looked at Ashley with wide eyes and waited for her response.

For a moment, Ashley didn't know what to say because she still thought that she might be dreaming. Looking around, she saw some other fairies making their way to school. Her spirit lightened, and a smile grew on her beautiful face at knowing that Brenna really wanted to be friends.

"Do you know, my mom and dad told me last night that I would make a friend soon? Yes! I want to be your friend!" Ashley replied excitedly.

"Yay!" Brenna exclaimed. The two fairies spun around in the air together, creating a blur of yellow and purple.

"Brenna, why didn't you tell me that you wanted to be friends?" Ashley asked when they finished twirling around in the air. It was Brenna who now looked shy and embarrassed.

"Well, I was scared to talk to you. I am a little shy about talking to others."

"I'm shy too," Ashley said. "Why did you say something now?"

"I was speaking with my parents last night and they told me I am brave and if I really wanted something, I should do it. So I asked you to be my friend because I know I am strong and brave." Brenna replied with a big smile on her pretty face.

Ashley had a beautiful smile on her face too and said, "My mom and dad told me something like that too." The girls both lit up and flew around the little patch they were in.

"Come, let's go play in the garden by the school before class starts," Brenna said. Both she and Ashley flew as fast as they could to the garden just outside the school hall.

As they arrived, the two fairies smiled at each other and made their way to the playground. Ashley felt thrilled as she played with her new friend. She was proud of being herself and making a friend, just like her parents had told her. Ashley now understood that being beautiful and strong made life better and that she didn't have to change to make friends.

That day, Ashley and Brenna became best friends who taught each other how to be beautiful and brave.

You are magical.
Don't forget that!

Faithful Rosie

Claire rode her bicycle down the street with the fall breeze behind her. She knew not to go too far; her parents said she could ride by herself as long as she didn't ride too far from the house.

Claire pedaled up and down thinking about all the things that she would do at her birthday party that weekend. She would finally be turning 10, and along with the mark of double digits, Claire could finally have a sleepover like she had always wanted. They were going to watch movies, eat a lot of pizza and candy, and stay up all night! Claire was really excited at what was to come and couldn't wait for the weekend to arrive.

As she made another turn to go down the street, Claire's mom stood on the sidewalk and called her to come inside. It had gotten dark, so she thought she was out there for a long time. As much as she didn't want to go inside after spending most of her day at school, Claire stored her bicycle in the garage and walked in the house.

"Claire, sweetie?" her mom called as Claire stepped into the kitchen. She saw her mom making her favorite meal of spaghetti, which made her excited all over again.

"Spaghetti and meatballs!" she exclaimed, and her mother let out a small chuckle.

"Of course! How else are we supposed to celebrate your birthday week without your favorite meal?" Claire's mom had a big smile on her face as she put the finishing touches on the delicious meal.

"Where's Dad?" Claire questioned, standing by the counter and trying—unsuccessfully—to pinch some cheese before her mother saw.

"Claire! Have you washed your hands?" Seeing her unsuccessful attempt at stealing cheese, Claire's mom scooped it up and placed the cheese far away from her daughter.

"Your father is going to be home soon. Go wash your hands and set the table for dinner," her mother instructed.

With a guilty smile at being caught, Claire silently made her way to the bathroom to wash up for dinner. By the time she set up the last place setting, her father had arrived.

"Daddy!" Claire ran into her father's arms as soon as he stepped into the kitchen.

"There's my princess!" He hugged her tight to him and, with Claire in his arms, went to say hello to her mom.

"How was school today, princess?" They had all taken their seats at the table when her dad started the conversation.

"Good!" Claire responded. "All my friends are so excited about the sleepover this weekend. It's going to be the best birthday ever!" Claire jumped up and down in her seat while her parents smiled at their excited child.

"What about you, sweetie? Are you excited about it?" Claire's mother jokingly asked.

"Of course! But, I'm more excited about tomorrow!"

"Tomorrow? What could be happening tomorrow?" Her dad asked, pretending like he didn't know what tomorrow was.

"My birthday, Daddy! You know that, right?" It shocked Claire that her father wouldn't remember her birthday. But when she saw the smile on her dad's face, she knew he was joking with her.

"Don't worry, princess. I will never forget your birthday. Speaking of which, your mother and I have a surprise for you after dinner."

"Really? What is it?" she excitedly asked.

"Well, it wouldn't be much of a surprise if we told you, now would it?" her mom stated.

Knowing what her mom said was true, Claire nodded her head and continued to eat her dinner as fast as she could. She was the first one finished, and as much as she wanted to know what the surprise was, Claire patiently waited for her parents to finish as well.

Finally, after cleaning everything up, they climbed into the car and left the house. As they were driving, Claire tried to think of all the places that they could be going. It wasn't for frozen yogurt as that was on the other side of town. And it wasn't to her grandparents' house as they just passed their street. She really couldn't think of any other place it could be, but that didn't mean that her excitement was fading. In fact, it made it all that more wonderful!

"Are you ready?" Claire's mother turned to face her with a beautiful smile on her face. Claire stared at her mom and thought about how pretty she was. Smiling, she nodded her head. Claire unbuckled herself to jump out of the car as soon as her dad said

she could.

"What is this place?" she asked, while looking around.

"Remember when you asked for a dog from the shelter?" Claire turned to her dad and stared at both her parents with hope in her eyes.

"Yeah?"

"I have a friend who works here, and she said that we could come now for you to choose which dog you want." At her mother's words, Claire ran up to hug them.

"I'm really getting a dog? " she asked, and they said yes.

"Thank you!" Claire said excitedly.

The family of three made their way into the shelter building and met with her mom's friend. She showed them to the area with all the dogs but Claire cried at seeing them.

"What's wrong, princess?" her father kneeled down to look into Claire's tearful eyes.

"It's just so sad that they all don't have nice homes. Can we take them all, Daddy?"

Listening to his daughter's request, Claire's dad pulled her into a hug and said, "Unfortunately, we can't. But I promise we will do everything we can to find good homes for them."

After father and daughter released each other from their hug, Claire walked down the aisle and pet all the dogs. Toward the middle area, she spotted a small black dog sitting right at the gate staring up at her. Claire bent down to pet the sweet dog, who immediately rolled over for a tummy scratch.

"Her name's Rosie and she's eight years old," her mom's friend said as she bent down to pet the dog as well.

"She's really pretty," Claire said as she continued to pet the black dog. She felt something in her heart, but wanted to look at the other dogs before deciding. Claire stood up and started walking again, but Rosie followed her and whined when Claire left her sight. She came back to the little dog and knew she loved Rosie already.

"I choose Rosie." With the excitement and love of adopting a pet, it seemed like time passed by quickly. Soon, Claire found herself cuddled up with Rosie in her bed. Her parents sat on either side of her and talked about what responsibilities she now had with Rosie.

"You have to take her for a walk every day. Make sure that she always has food and water. Clean up after her and be the best

friend that Rosie has ever had." Claire was already agreeing with everything that they said and knew that she would always look after her dog, no matter what.

"I promise I will."

"Happy Birthday, Claire." With those last words, her parents turned off the light and Claire fell asleep with Rosie in her arms.

From that day on, nothing could ever separate Claire and Rosie. Wherever Claire went, Rosie would follow, and she did her best to make sure her dog knew she was loved. Claire took her role as Rosie's friend and guardian seriously. She grew every day with what she learned while caring for her wonderful friend.

Two years later, Claire celebrated her 12th birthday with Rosie by her side. She thought about their bond and how there was nothing as special as that. Claire ran around the backyard with Rosie following her every step. The fall sun shone on the pair, creating a halo of light.

Rosie and Claire shared a devoted faithfulness and an unending love.

Be caring

The Lemonade Stand

On a sunny afternoon in July, Abigail and her mother, Julie, sat together by the poolside. It had been a boiling day, as it normally is in the peak summer months. Julie thought it was a good idea for the two girls to have a mother-daughter pool day.

Abby's mom stretched on the lawn chair while she played with her toys on the pool step. Abby loved her toys, which comprised her two mermaid dolls and a bunch of small swimming animals. They sat in companionable silence as Abby created many worlds for her swimming friends. In one world, the pink mermaid found a sea turtle that needed help. In another, the blue mermaid hurt her tail and the pink one made her feel better. Thinking about her different stories, Abigail remembered something that she had forgotten.

"Mom?" she called out to Julie, who put her book down and faced her 11-year-old daughter.

"Yes, Abby?"

"There's a new doll that I saw at the store with Grandma the other day. It was really pretty," the little girl said. Abby had stopped playing with her toys and swam to the pool edge near her mother.

"Oh really? What did it look like?" Julie bent forward with her arms on her knees and listened to Abby's detailed description of the doll.

"She had long hair, longer than yours, Mom! And a white shirt

that had a picture of a unicorn on it. She also had rainbow hair!" Abigail exclaimed.

"Rainbow hair? Wow!" her mom replied, smiling at her daughter as she excitedly talked about the doll.

"Yes! And it was all the colors too! Purple, pink, blue, yellow, and green. All of them! She was really pretty." Abby sighed, dreaming about the doll that she really wanted.

"I asked Grandma if we could get it and she said I had to ask you and Dad." Julie looked to see her daughter begging silently for the doll. All she could do was smile at Abby.

"Well, I have to speak to your father first and we'll let you know, okay?" Her mother moved a piece of stray hair off of Abby's face and gave her cheek a gentle rub.

"Okay, Mom." Abigail swam off and once again, created a whole new world for her and her toys.

Not too long after that, Julie got her daughter out of the pool and in the shower before dinner. Abby played with her other dolls in the shower, then climbed out and into her pink pajamas. As her mother was brushing out Abby's hair, the garage door opened to reveal Abigail's older brother, Samuel, and her father,

Jack.

Sam had just finished a baseball game and couldn't stop talking about it. Luckily, they had won and would play in the next round. Abby knew that her brother really loved baseball, and she liked to play softball as well.

Over dinner, they shared stories about everyone's day and Abby told her father about the special doll that she wanted. Jack said he would have to speak with her mom and they would do that while the children watched a movie. It was a Friday night, which meant Samuel and Abigail could pick a movie to watch and eat popcorn, too!

"Let's watch School of Rock!" Sam shouted as he and Abby raced to the sofa.

"No! We always watch that. I want to watch something else," Abigail whined. She jumped onto the sofa and the two children fought until they agreed on a movie. Star Wars won the debate and for the next couple of hours, there was peace in the household.

It was finally time for bed, so Abigail's parents tucked her in and said that they had spoken about the doll.

"Abby," her father began. "We know you really want that doll. But since you're eleven now, your mom and I think you should earn it."

Confused, Abigail looked between her parents and asked, "What do you mean?"

"Instead of us buying you the doll, we think you should find a way to get the money you need to buy it for yourself." It was her mother's turn to explain the idea to their daughter.

"Do you mean I should do more chores or something?" Abby

felt sleepy and pulled the blanket further up.

"Something like that. Or you could think of another way to earn the money. But your mom and I have to approve it first." When Jack finished speaking, he placed a kiss on his tired daughter's forehead and Abby's parents said goodnight. That night, Abigail dreamed of fancy kingdoms filled with rainbows and chores.

***

Saturday morning was the busiest time of the weekend for the family. Sam and Jack rushed from football practice to golf camp while the girls went to ballet class and grocery shopping. This left little time for Abby to think of a way that she could earn money for her doll. But it was never too far from her mind. She thought she could do chores, but what else was there to do after the ones she already had to do?

It was lunchtime, and they all met up at the local pizzeria. Sam was talking about sports when Abigail remembered a story that her mom told her a while ago.

"Oh, I know!" At her sudden outburst, her parents and brother faced her with confused looks.

"You know what?" Sam asked as he dipped his pizza into some ranch sauce and took a bite.

"I know how to earn money for my doll," she stated proudly.

"Really? And what did you think of?" Her father asked. He, too, took a bite of his food.

"I'm going to do a lemonade stand. Like Mom did when she was my age, right Mom?"

"That's right, I did. I think it's a wonderful idea!"

"I do, too," Jack added. Her parents agreed that this would be the best way for Abby to earn some money. They finished their lunch and the mother-daughter duo stopped by the store for some supplies.

That afternoon was spent with everyone helping Abigail set up her lemonade stand. They decided she would start selling it the next day on the walking trail near their house. Her father and brother helped build the stand while Abby and her mom made the lemonade to chill overnight.

Abigail was really excited to begin her adventure of selling

lemonade and it showed, as she couldn't stop talking about it. She even phoned both her grandparents to let them know what she was going to do. Abby and Sam's grandparents were really proud of the idea and promised to stop by for a cup of lemonade the following day.

Before she knew it, Abby was set up on the trail and ready to start the day. Sam spent some time selling lemonade with her until he left to play with his friends. The first few hours were slow and few people bought from her. But as lunchtime came and people were spending the day outdoors, Abby's lemonade soon became a hit!

As promised, her grandparents came to support her and bought some lemonade. Lunch came and went, and so did the people. Abby only needed to sell one more cup of lemonade to buy the doll. But with each passing minute and no one stopping by her stand, she became upset. Just then, a small girl walked by, holding hands with her mom. Abby recognized her from school, although the girl was in a younger grade.

"Mommy, look! Can we get some lemonade?" The small girl asked excitedly.

"I don't have any money, sweetie. I'm sorry." Abby watched the scene in front of her and saw the little girl getting upset. She was about to give her a cup for free when the little girl spoke up once more.

"Oh! I found this quarter on the trail. Do you think I can get some with it?" she asked her mother.

Abby sold the girl a cup of lemonade for that quarter and with the help of her parents buying some lemonade too, she finally had enough for her doll!

The next day, Julie drove Abigail and Sam to the store. Abby was really excited about getting the doll and ran toward the aisle as soon as she could. She grabbed the box and turned to smile at her mother when she saw the same little girl from the day before. She and her mom were looking at the dolls too. Sam spent some more time looking for the right thing to buy with his money, so Abby stood with their mom and watched the other people.

"Mommy, please, can I get it? Pretty please?" The small girl begged her mom.

"Oh, sweetie. I wish we could, but Mommy and Daddy don't have the money for it this time. Maybe next month, alright?" Her mom wiped the tears from the girl's face and Abby looked down at the doll in her hands.

Abby thought back to the previous day when the little girl gave her the only quarter she had. If it wasn't for her, Abby wouldn't be buying her toy today. Thinking about what she wanted to do, Abigail and Sam checked out the toys that they wanted. However, before they could leave, Abby asked if they could wait for a minute. Not telling her mom what she wanted to do, Abby made her way to the little girl when they passed by.

"Here you go." Abigail gave the little girl her doll, feeling happy when she gave Abby a smile.

"Are you giving this to me?"

"Yes, I want you to have it," she replied.

After their mothers made sure that it was fine for the little girl to take the doll, the two of them thanked Abby for her kindness before everyone drove home. Over dinner that night, Julie told

Jack what had happened and Abigail's parents told her how proud they were of her and how much they loved her.

"Abby? Can we talk to you?" her dad asked. Nodding her head, Abby climbed into her bed with her parents smiling on either side of her.

"Because of what you did for that little girl today, we are going to buy you another doll." Abby looked at the smiles on their faces and she smiled, too.

"Thank you Mom and Dad, but I didn't do it for that."

"We know, sweetie. But can you tell us why you thought of it?" Her mom asked, brushing back her daughter's hair.

"I saw how sad the little girl was and her mom said they didn't have money. I wanted to make her happy."

"That was really kind of you, sweetie."

"Thanks, Mom. But I don't want you guys to buy me the doll."

"Why not?" her dad questioned.

"Because I enjoyed doing the lemonade stand and earning my own money. I want to do it again!" Abby smiled as she said this. Julie and Jack looked at each other with proud smiles on their faces, kissed their daughter goodnight, and left her to sleep.

Abigail had dreams filled with lemons and rainbows. Even in her sleep, she was excited to begin again.

Be kind

The Fighting Royals

In a kingdom far, far away—but not that far away—there lived a prince and princess who, to the outside world, seemed to be the perfect brother and sister. However, the prince and princess often fought with each other. Sometimes it would be so bad that their parents, the king and queen, didn't know how to help them.

Then one stormy day in the kingdom, the two children were stuck inside and only had each other to play with. Once again, instead of playing fairly, they started arguing.

"Give it back, you little turd!" Prince Henry exclaimed. He pulled his toy back toward him after his little sister, Princess Elizabeth, had taken it from his side of the room.

"But you said I could play with it!" Princess Elizabeth shouted back. She thought her brother was always unfair to her just because he was two years older. He felt he could do whatever he wanted.

Whenever Elizabeth pulled, Henry tugged back in his direction. And like this, they went back-and-forth for a while. Both the prince and princess were shouting at each other

when their father found them.

"Children! Settle down!" The king commanded. At the sound of their father's voice, both Henry and Elizabeth let go of the toy and it dropped to the ground. Slowly turning to face him, the royal children showed embarrassed faces.

"Why do you two insist on fighting all the time?" Their father asked as he made his way into the playroom. He stood in front of his children with a tired expression.

"She started it!"

"He started it!"

They both exclaimed simultaneously, then, once again started fighting.

Annoyed with having to break up their constant fights, the king took a seat on the sofa in the corner and called his children to sit with him.

Henry sat on the left side of his father while Elizabeth sat on his right. They gave each other a funny look before finally settling into silence.

"What happened here?" the king asked.

Both children looked at their father without speaking. The king waited for someone to say something and kept quiet until one of them spoke up.

"Elizabeth took my toy without asking." Henry finally said and stared at her with a mean look on his face.

"He said I could play with it and it was just lying on the floor!" Elizabeth exclaimed. She too was upset, as her brother always

blamed everything on her.

"Just because I left it on the floor doesn't mean that you get to take it whenever you want. You're such a brat! I hate playing with you!"

"You're so mean to me. I don't like playing with you either! I wish I never have to play with you again!" Elizabeth sat with her arms crossed and her lips pouted. Their father let out a tired sigh as the queen appeared in the doorway.

"Are you two still fighting even with your father in the room?" The queen asked from her spot by the door. Henry and Elizabeth immediately stopped fighting and all three of them looked at her.

"Do you have anything to say for yourselves? This room is a complete disaster and I'm tired of listening to you children always arguing. You need to sort this out before both of you are punished." The queen looked at the king and gave him a slight nod of the head. "I think it's time you told them the story," she said before turning around and leaving them in silence once more.

"What is Mother speaking about Father?" Henry questioned, puzzled.

Again, the king let out an exhausted sigh while rubbing his eyes with one hand. Their father didn't speak for a while, which left Henry and Elizabeth to think about what their mother said.

Elizabeth looked around the playroom and thought about the mess that she and her brother had made. *Henry is going to make me clean up by myself,* she thought to herself.

"Do you know," the king began. "When I was your age, my sister and I fought a lot too."

Henry and Elizabeth were shocked when their father told them this, as they didn't know he had a sister.

"You have a sister, Father?" Henry asked, curious about what had happened to her.

"Was she older than you, Daddy?" Elizabeth asked.

Her father looked at her and replied, "She was younger than me. Like you and your brother."

Henry and Elizabeth looked at each other as their father said this.

"What happened to her?" Elizabeth asked, interested in her father's story.

"Well, one summer we were fighting a lot like you two. My father told us he loved us but he had to send my sister to my aunt and uncle's town because of the fighting."

"And then?" Henry asked as he was more confused than before.

"We didn't see each other for a long time and I became very sad. I missed my sister dearly. It made me think about all the times that we fought and how we could've spent that time playing. How we could've loved each other more."

"But Daddy, how come we haven't met your sister?" Elizabeth asked. Her father looked at her for a moment, thinking over his words.

"When we got older, I met your mother, and we became the royals of this kingdom. My sister and her husband became the royals of another kingdom. This place is so far away, you can't see it over the horizon. So, I haven't seen my sister in many years and I miss her a lot."

All three of them sat in silence for a while before Henry finally asked what had been on his mind. "Father, are you telling us that you're going to send Elizabeth away?"

"Oh! No, no, no!" the king laughed. "I could never send my little girl away," he said as he pulled her into a big hug. Elizabeth was happy that her father had said no and hugged him back just as tightly.

"What I'm trying to tell you is that not everyone gets to spend as much time with their loved one as you do. Hearing you two fight makes your mother and I very sad. Especially me because I haven't seen my sister in many years and I want you two to have a strong bond that will never break."

Henry now understood what his father was feeling and felt bad for fighting with Elizabeth all the time. She was his little sister, who he always needed to protect and love.

"I'm sorry, Elizabeth. I'm sorry that I haven't been a good big brother to you and I will try harder. I do love you, little sis," Henry said.

"I love you too, Henry. I'm sorry for everything. I don't want to be a brat to you. You're my big brother." They both got up and hugged each other while the king looked at them with a loving smile.

"That's what I like to hear, my two dearest loves. I am so proud of you. Your mom and I love you both." With that, the king got up and left the children to play.

Prince Henry and Princess Elizabeth spent the rest of the day playing together. It surprised all the people in the castle that they hadn't fought again.

Love your brothers and sisters

Championship? Champion!

"The bases are loaded, Molly." Coach Anderson said as Molly was warming up. It was game day—championship game day—and they were in the last inning. The game was tied with her team having three batters on all bases.

"You're up next. You think you can hit a big one and bring it all home?" Molly's coach asked as he kneeled down to look her in the eyes. Molly was focused on the pitcher's mound, where the other team was discussing strategy.

"Molly?" Coach Anderson called out again. Breaking her focus on the pitcher and bringing it to her coach, Molly stared into eyes very similar to her own.

"Yes, coach?" she replied, picking up her helmet and tossing it from hand to hand.

"I don't want to put a lot of pressure on you. This is a highly stressful moment. Are you sure you can do this?"

"You don't think I can do it, coach?" Molly looked at the person she trusted the most and feared that he didn't believe in her as much as he said he did.

"No, never. I do believe you can do it, Molly. I'm just concerned about your arm. This is the first time you're going to have to really use it since the accident." Coach Anderson looked at Molly's right arm and saw that she was unknowingly rubbing it.

Molly followed his gaze and looked down at her arm as well. It didn't hurt anymore, having been healed for a while now. But the

memories of the accident and the feeling of the pain were still fresh in her mind.

"Coach, can you call a timeout? I just need a few more minutes." At Molly's request, Coach Anderson spoke to the umpire who called another timeout, the last one of the game.

Molly took a seat in a shaded area near her team's dugout and breathed in deeply. The memories from the accident came rushing back to her, and she started rubbing her arm again.

***

It was the first game of the under 12 softball league season and Molly had been really excited. This year was her turn to be the star. As the oldest on the team and the captain, she knew she had a lot to do. Softball was her favorite sport, and she wanted to play it professionally. Everyone told her that she could be the best player one day—that was how good she was. But Molly didn't see it like that. She practiced every day to get better and her coach stood by her side through everything.

Molly played the position of second base on the field and she was the fourth batter in the lineup. At this particular time, she was in her field position, ready for the next opposing batter to take her stance. There was a girl on first base and Molly kept her eye

on her while paying attention to the batter. She didn't want the girl to steal second.

The pitcher, Molly's best friend Stacey, lined up her pitch and threw the ball. The batter hit a fly ball, coming straight toward Molly. It was probably the easiest catch she'd had the entire game, and the batter was out. But the play wasn't over yet. Molly turned to the girl running from first to second base, ready to tag her out. As she turned, though, the girl ran into her and Molly went tumbling to the ground.

The shooting pain up her arm was the first thing she felt and Molly screamed. Her coach and many others rushed to her side; she couldn't make out what they were saying, the pain blinded her to everything. In a blur, they rushed Molly to the hospital where they found out she had broken her arm. It was no one's fault; she had just landed on it at the wrong angle.

Molly was sitting on the hospital bed when her coach came in. "Hey Molly. How are you feeling?"

She shrugged her shoulders in answer; the pain now numb after the doctor had attended to her.

"Coach?"

"Yeah?" Coach Anderson grabbed a chair and placed it by her bedside. Sitting down, he looked at her, waiting for Molly to continue.

"Did I tag the girl?" At her question, her coach laughed a little before giving her a small smile.

"Yes, you did."

**

"Molly? Are you ready?" Coach Anderson asked as he came to her side. She looked up at him with memories playing in her eyes. Today would be the first time she has played since the beginning of the season and everyone was counting on her.

You can do it, she thought to herself. Nodding her head and taking her coach's outstretched hand, Molly pulled herself up and walked over to her helmet and bat. She set her helmet on her head, picked up her bat, and turned to walk toward the umpire and catcher.

"Molly?" Turning around, she saw her coach giving her a big smile. "I believe in you. You're the best player on the team. You can do it." Giving him a smile back, she took another deep breath and stepped into the box.

She took her position, stared at the pitcher, and waited for the ball. The first pitch came flying at her, but instead of swinging to

hit, Molly stood there in shock.

"Strike one!" The umpire called out.

Molly took a step back and refocused her energy. It was almost like her arm refused to swing. *Come on, Molly, you can do this. Just swing the bat and hit the ball. You just need to bring one player home for the win*, she thought to herself as she stepped back in and took her stance for the next pitch.

"Strike two!" the umpire called out once again. Molly heard the cheers of the opposing team and took another deep breath in.

"Come on, Molly. You can do it!" She looked up at her coach again and then at her teammates who were all cheering for her.

"Let's go, Molly. Let's go!" they chanted, and she smiled at them.

She stepped back in and slowed her breathing down. *Okay*, she thought. *One more hit. Win or lose, you still did your best.*

The pitcher threw the ball as she repeated that to herself, but this time, Molly swung her arm and hit high and far. She had hit the ball so far it became a home run, and the three other girls on the bases ran to the home plate as well.

They had won the game!

Everyone on her team was screaming and jumping around excitedly. Her coach came running up to her with a big smile on his face.

"I knew you could do it Molly!" He said. Molly didn't feel the excitement. All she felt was the pain in her arm.

"What's wrong?" Her coach asked with concern.

"It's my arm. It's hurting really bad." Molly was about to cry

because of the pain. Quickly, her coach spoke to his assistant and in the middle of the celebration, the two of them rushed to the hospital once again.

Molly felt scared, thinking that she had broken her arm again. She didn't know what she would do if she had. Before they knew it, they were at the hospital and sent Molly in for scans. They were waiting in the hospital room when the doctor came in. He smiled at Molly and her coach.

"Hi Molly, I'm Doctor Alex." Molly gave him a small smile in return and looked at her coach. He grabbed her uninjured hand and squeezed it in support.

"Your arm isn't broken. It's just sprained because you haven't used it much and it isn't used to swinging a bat."

Doctor Alex told her coach what they would need to do to get it strong again before leaving the room.

"Coach?" Molly quietly called out.

"Molly, the game is over. You can call me Dad again." She looked into her father's eyes.

"Will I be able to play softball again?" she asked, scared that the answer would be no and that she would have to give up the one thing she always dreamed of.

"Yes, baby. It's going to heal and we're going to train before the next season starts."

"Dad, the team did a great job this year. They got to the championship without me and I am so proud of my friends."

"They had an amazing captain. You were there for every game, cheering them on even when you were sore. Your friends love

you, Molly. And so do I."

Her teammates came to visit her that afternoon and they gave Molly her trophy. She didn't have to stay in the hospital; they were just waiting for the doctor to say she could go home. Her friends left shortly after, saying that they would see her at the victory party the team was having at their favorite pizza place.

Molly closed her eyes to rest as the door closed behind her friends and her father smiled. He was happy she could play again. She was also happy that she was a part of an amazing softball team.

Believe in yourself

Learning Something New

Olivia looked at the piece of paper in front of her. Being in fifth grade meant everyone had to do weekly tests. This week's test was on history, but she was never interested in it, so she hadn't studied for it—like her teacher said she should—and now Olivia was stuck staring at the test. She didn't know what to write.

Luckily for her, she could still remember some things that they learned in class. Olivia could fill out most of the questions because of that. But she knew she would not be getting the best mark. Her teacher collected their tests and said they would get them back by the end of the day. As they were sent out for recess, Olivia joined her friends, Emma and Mia.

"Hi Olivia! How was your test?" Emma asked. Her light brown hair was tied in a high ponytail and it swung down her back with every step she took.

"It wasn't great," Olivia replied, feeling embarrassed.

"Oh, well, that's okay. History isn't that great," Mia said as the three girls made their way to the swing set. This is what they did every recess if there wasn't anything else to do. For a while, Olivia didn't say much as she thought about what her parents were going to say when she gave them her test.

She knew they wouldn't be proud of her marks. *Mom and Dad are probably going to ground me*, she thought to herself. As their break went on, Olivia put the test out of her mind and tried to have as much fun with her friends as she could. She was certain

the only time she would see them for a while was at school.

Recess finally ended, and the girls went back to class. The rest of the day passed by with nothing special in the classroom. It was now their last class, which was the one subject Olivia wasn't looking forward to—History. She looked back at her friends as their teacher gave the tests back. She saw smiles spread onto both Emma and Mia's faces and knew they got good marks. They had studied for the test.

Olivia had her head facing the floor when her teacher stopped by her desk and kneeled down.

"Olivia, did you study for this test?" Without looking up or saying a word, she shook her head.

"Look at me, Olivia." Slowly, she turned to face her teacher and saw the disappointment on her face.

"I know you can do better than this. You just have to study.

As you get older and go into higher grades, the tests are going to become more difficult. You need to learn how to best prepare for them now."

"Yes, Miss Tanner," Olivia quietly replied. Her teacher placed her test down on the desk and continued handing out the rest. She secretly turned over the page and was shocked at the grade she had gotten. Her parents would definitely not be happy with that.

The bell rang, signaling the end of school, and Olivia once again walked out with her friends.

"What did you guys get on your tests?" she asked as they walked out of the school. They all lived on the same street and always walked home together.

"I got an A!"

"So did I!" Emma and Mia gave each other a high-five and looked over at Olivia.

"What did you get?" Mia asked, her blue eyes staring at Olivia.

"I got a D."

"Oh." Mia responded and looked away from her. The three girls walked in silence for a while before Emma spoke up.

"If you need help to study for next week's test, we can help you!"

"Thank you, guys. But I don't think we would be able to see each other after school for a while. My parents are seriously going to ground me."

Both Mia and Emma agreed with what she said before walking to their own homes. Oliva hadn't been wrong. That night, her

parents grounded her for two weeks. They also said she needed to study for every test she had. Olivia felt so embarrassed about her grades that she made the choice to study really hard from then on. She wanted her parents and her teacher to all be proud of her. So that is what she did.

For the next week, Olivia spent most of her time studying her school books. The following week's test was on Mathematics which was another subject she didn't like. There were a lot of things she needed to remember for the test, and Olivia thought she would not do as well as she wanted.

That Friday morning, Olivia sat at her desk feeling a little ready and a lot nervous. *Did I study enough? Did I study the right things?* These were the thoughts running through her mind as the test was placed down in front of her. An hour later, after giving it her best, she handed the test in and went to play with her friends outside. The day continued the same as the previous week and soon Olivia was looking at her teacher as she handed the Math tests out.

"Olivia." Miss Tanner stopped by her desk once more.

"Yes, Miss Tanner?" Her teacher bent down and looked Olivia in the eyes.

"Did you study for this test like I suggested last week?" At her question, Olivia felt disappointed in herself. If her teacher was asking her this question, then that means she didn't do as well as she had hoped.

"I promise you, Miss Tanner. I studied so hard and made sure I remembered all of it, but there were some things I didn't remember." Olivia was sad that her hard work wasn't good enough, and she was waiting for her teacher to give her the bad news.

"I see." Miss Tanner looked at the tests in her hand and carefully placed Olivia's on her desk. "Well, whatever you did Olivia, it was very good." With a smile, her teacher left her desk and Olivia stared at the piece of paper. Slowly turning it over, hope filled her heart.

***

Emma, Mia, and Olivia were nearly on their street when Emma asked, "Olivia, are you still grounded?"

"Yeah, I have one more week to go."

"Oh. What did you guys get for your tests? I got an A again," Mia said proudly.

"I got an A as well," Emma said.

"Wow, you guys are so smart!" Olivia responded, proud that her best friends were getting good grades.

"What did you get, Olivia?" Emma asked quietly.

"I got a B!" she said with a smile. All the girls jumped for joy when they heard her grade. Even Olivia's parents were happy for her. She was so happy with her grade that Olivia studied even harder for the following week's test.

This one was going to be about Science, which was her hardest subject to remember. That didn't stop Olivia, though. She studied all week long and tried her best to understand the subject as best she could.

The time came to take the test and as nervous as she was about it, Olivia was happy with the work that she had done. For the first time, Olivia didn't sit staring at the page because she didn't know the answers. She spent the full hours answering all the questions she could without stopping. She handed in her test and went to recess. Olivia enjoyed her break this time because she wasn't worried about her grade. Even if she didn't get an A, she would be happy with a B.

At the end of the day, Olivia was excited to get her test back. She looked at her friends and saw they were happy with their marks. Obviously, Emma and Mia had gotten A's again. Her teacher was coming toward her desk but passed it without giving her the test back. Confused, Olivia stared at her teacher as she finished handing out the papers and stood in front of the class. Olivia put her hand up to ask a question.

"Olivia," her teacher called.

"Miss Tanner, I didn't get my test back."

"You didn't? Let me see. Class, your scores were really great on this test. Most of you got an A, but one of you had the highest score out of the entire fifth grade!"

Excited whispers started at those words. Olivia still didn't have her test, but she knew it wouldn't be her, anyway. She sighed and waited for Miss Tanner to finish so that she could get her own test back.

"Olivia!" She was surprised when her teacher called out her name. *Why is she calling me?* Olivia thought. Miss Tanner came to her desk and placed the test in front of her.

"You got an A+ and the highest grade. Well done, Olivia. I'm proud of you!" Miss Tanner said. The class cheered for Olivia; Emma and Mia were clapping the loudest.

Olivia couldn't believe that she got the highest score! Her parents were going to be so proud of her and maybe they would go out for ice cream as a reward. All of Olivia's hard work and determination paid off. She really could do it if she put in the work.

Always keep improving

Mystery Forest

"Dad? Can I go buy some candy?" Beth pulled on her father's hand that was wrapped around her own. She looked around the busy main street and spotted the candy store right next door to the bicycle shop. That is where her father wanted to go, but Beth always got bored when she was there.

"Sure, but remember to be safe and come straight to the store when you're done." Beth agreed with her dad as he gave her some money. With a hug, off she went.

Beth skipped down the sidewalk, her blonde hair falling into her face, and the white dress she wore was swaying in the breeze. She liked it when her parents said she could do things on her own. She was growing up and knew to always be safe and stay close, no matter what.

Before entering the store, she eyed all the different types of candy that were on display in the window. There were lollipops so big that they looked like golf balls, bubblegum of every flavor, and her personal favorite—the big collection of gummy bears!

She was just about to step through the door when she heard her name being called.

"Beth!" She turned toward the caller and saw her father standing at the foot of the bicycle shop entrance.

"Yes, Dad?" Beth called in return.

"Remember to come straight back to me the minute you're done. I'll be waiting here for you. And tell Mrs. Grace, I say hello."

With a smile and a promise to do as he said, Beth turned to the entrance but stopped short. Normally there was a big toy machine just outside the door, but today there wasn't. Finding this strange, Beth scanned the outside of the store one more time and, seeing as everything looked normal, opened the door and stepped inside.

Except, things were not normal inside the candy shop. Actually, it wasn't the candy shop anymore.

Beth had stepped into a forest of green trees and chirping birds. Confused about what she was doing there, Beth surely thought that she must be dreaming. Taking a step back and turning to leave, she found the door had disappeared. There was a wooden board in its place that read, "Mystery Forest: Home to Majestic Creatures."

She wandered in a circle, looking up at the tall trees and down at the glowing ground. When she spotted the glittering floor, Beth really thought that she was imagining things. But seeing as

there was no way to leave the area she was standing in, she thought that there must be some other way out deeper in the forest.

Beth took a deep breath and reminded herself that she was a brave girl who could do anything she put her mind to. With that thought, she put one foot in front of the other and carefully journeyed through the woods.

The first few steps she took were uneventful, with only the sounds of nature following her. Beth thought about the magical animals that were said to be in the forest. *What type of animals could they be? And where were they?* she wondered.

It was like the forest could read her mind because as she rounded the huge, old tree, Beth spotted a small creature hopping from one red mushroom to another. She stopped in her tracks and held her breath, afraid of what might happen if the creature saw her.

But nothing happened. The creature stopped and considered Beth with a playful but confused expression. She considered the creature as well. In the stillness of the cool forest, Beth could see that the tiny creature was actually a fairy!

Beth loved the stories that were filled with fairies and a smile came to her face. Seeing the change in Beth's mood, the fairy smiled at her as well and continued on its way.

Finally releasing the breath she had been holding, Beth let out a laugh and immediately covered her mouth with her hand. Her laugh echoed throughout the forest and the volume frightened her. Beth searched for the fairy from where she stood but couldn't find anything. After standing still for a few moments longer, she continued down the path.

There were so many different creatures hiding out in this magical place. She spotted some gnomes enjoying an afternoon picnic and a few fairies picking berries. Her eyes were wide open to the magic in the air, so she wasn't paying attention to where she was going and ran into something very hard and very big.

Beth looked up at the giant creature she ran into and saw that it was a unicorn! It was white with silver hair and its horn seemed to glow even brighter than the forest floor. She was so shocked to see an actual unicorn that she didn't see it turn its head to face her.

The unicorn was big and beautiful, but Beth felt slightly afraid. It took a step toward her, then another, and another one. Afraid that the unicorn would hurt her, Beth turned around and ran back the way she came.

Beth didn't have to turn around to see if the unicorn was following her because she could hear its heavy galloping behind her. Closer and closer it came, while Beth tried to run faster!

Soon, she felt a presence beside her and turned to face the unicorn. The first thought Beth had was that it was going to run into her, but then she saw the smile on the unicorn's face. She then knew that it would not hurt her. Instead, it wanted to play.

Laughing at her silly thoughts, Beth had one moment left to enjoy it before she turned back and saw the name board. There

was no going back, as she was sure she would hit it. Closing her eyes and preparing herself for impact, Beth was ready to hit the board. But instead of running into the solid piece of wood, she ran out onto the sidewalk.

Quickly standing up and looking for the unicorn, Beth noticed that everything was normal again; some people looked worried about her fall. She made sure to tell them she was alright and walked back into the candy store. Wanting to go back into the forest, she was disappointed to find the regular old candy store instead.

Confused once more about what had happened, Beth greeted Mrs. Grace and picked out her candy. As she was paying for it, Mrs. Grace smiled at her and asked, "Is something on your mind, dear?"

Beth looked at the beautifully aged face and replied, "Mrs. Grace? Have you heard of the Mystery Forest?"

"Oh, no, dear. I haven't." Taking the bag she held out, Beth nodded her head and continued to walk toward the door.

"Oh Beth, dear?" Turning toward Mrs. Grace, Beth was shocked at what she had to say.

"Only the bravest girls of them all get to run with unicorns." With a wink and a smile, Mrs. Grace went into the back room, leaving Beth staring after her. *What a curious afternoon*, she thought.

Birthday Cupcakes

Hailey, Hannah, and Leah were standing around the kitchen table. They had their mother's recipe box spilled over the counter, searching for the perfect one to make for her birthday next week. The three sisters wanted to practice it before their mom's birthday so that they could make sure the cupcakes were good.

"What about the vanilla caramel ones?" Hailey, the oldest of the three, picked up that cupcake recipe and started to read it.

"No, Dad likes the caramel ones more than Mom and it's Mom's birthday, so we should make something that she really likes," Hannah said, climbing onto one of the bar stools to look at the recipes more closely.

Leah was the youngest at 10 years old and was already sitting on the counter. She wasn't as tall as her sisters, so she had to climb up there to see everything. While Hannah and Hailey were talking about the caramel cupcakes, Leah remembered one that their mother really liked.

"Guys, what about those chocolate ones that Stella used to make?" Stella was their old babysitter and Leah remembered her special cupcakes that everyone loved. Their mom loved them the most.

"Oh, yeah!" Hailey said as she looked for that recipe card on the counter.

"Wasn't it something like a double-chocolate cupcake with chocolate frosting?" Hannah asked as she, too, looked for the card.

The three girls took their time to look for the recipe when Leah saw something sticking out from the bottom of the pile and pulled it out.

"I found it! I think we should make these." Handing the recipe card to her oldest sister, Leah excitedly climbed down from the counter and ran to the pantry. She wasn't sure about all the ingredients that were needed, but she knew that chocolate chips were on the list.

She opened the pantry door and saw the chocolate chip bag on the highest shelf. Leah started to climb the shelves when Hailey came in.

"Leah, let me get them down for you. You know Mom and Dad don't like it when you climb the shelves like that."

"No! I want to get them!" Leah shouted at her sister. Hailey left the pantry upset, and Leah finally grabbed the bag.

When she left the pantry, her two older sisters went inside to get the rest of what they needed. Leah could see that Hailey was still upset with her, but didn't say anything. Opening the bag, she started eating some chocolate chips.

"Leah, can you come help us get all the things we need, please?" Hannah asked when she carried out the flour.

"No, I'm busy," she said, putting a few more chocolate chips in her mouth.

Hannah stopped and looked at her. "Busy doing what? Eating the only chocolate chips we have to make this recipe twice?"

Nodding her head, Leah went back to eating the chocolate chips, and Hannah helped Hailey. She watched as her two older sisters got everything ready on the counter and pulled up a chair in front of the mixing bowls.

"Leah, what are you doing?" Hailey asked, stopping next to her climbing onto the chair.

"I'm getting ready to bake!" she said excitedly.

"I can see that, but there's no space for us to help."

"Why would you help? I'm doing this by myself." Leah grabbed the whisk and faced the counter laid out with all the ingredients.

"That's not how we're supposed to be doing this, Leah." Hannah said as she stood next to Hailey.

"Yeah, we said we would do it together for Mom." The two of them stared at her, waiting for an answer.

Leah ignored what they said and turned back to the counter. She was going to do this all by herself. She was a big girl and didn't need anyone's help.

"Leah! Did you hear us?" Hailey asked, which made Leah look at her.

"Yes, I did. But I don't want to do it with you. I want to do it all by myself."

"Fine! But when you need help, don't come and ask us." Hannah stormed off angrily and Leah looked at her oldest sister,

confused.

"What's her problem?"

"Her problem, Leah, is that we wanted to do this together to make Mom's birthday special. But no, like always, you have to do everything. It's really not nice and we don't like it when you behave this way." Hailey walked out as well, leaving Leah alone in the kitchen.

She was fine with it. She wanted to bake the cupcakes by herself so she was going to do it by herself. Leah picked up the recipe card and started to read what she had to do. The first step was to turn the oven on.

That was easy enough for her to do. It took her some time because she couldn't reach the buttons, but she eventually did it. Back on the chair by the mixing bowls, Leah mixed the cupcake batter. As time went on and a big mess was made, she began to think that it wasn't as easy as she thought it was. She accidentally dropped one of the dirty bowls on the floor and climbed off the chair to pick it up. When she stood up, Leah saw her mother standing in the doorway.

"What's going on here?" Her mom said, stepping closer to her.

"I'm practicing the cupcakes I wanted to make for you for your birthday." Leah placed the bowl in the kitchen sink and

climbed back onto the chair while her mom stood beside her and looked at the mess she had made.

"Oh? And how is that going?"

"Well, it's not as easy as I thought it would be." Leah looked at her mom, feeling embarrassed about the mess.

"Leah, weren't you and your sisters supposed to be making this together? Like you said you would?"

"I told them I wanted to make them myself, that I didn't want them to help."

"Why would you say that?"

Leah looked away from her mom and down at the flour sitting on the counter.

"I wanted to show you that I am a big girl and I wanted to make these extra special for you," she whispered without looking at her mom.

"Leah, look at me," her mom said. Leah slowly turned her head and faced her mom with tears in her eyes.

"Honey, the cupcakes are going to be special for me because my three daughters made them together. I love you all so much and I know you want to prove yourself. But Leah, sometimes the best way to show how grown up you are, is to let other people help you when you need it. How did your sisters feel when you said that to them?"

"I guess they were upset about it."

"I know it upset them. Go look outside and tell me what you see." Leah climbed off the chair once again and stared out the kitchen door. Her sisters were sitting at the picnic table looking

very sad.

"You see, Leah. Working together as a family and as friends is what makes things special. Do you understand?"

"Yes, Mom." Leah looked back outside and felt terrible for acting the way she did.

"Now, apologize to them. Maybe they'll come help you after that."

Leah listened to her mom and slowly walked outside. She stopped in front of the table and both sisters looked up at her. No one spoke for a few minutes.

"Hailey, Hannah," Leah began. "I'm really sorry for the way I acted. I just wanted to be big like you guys are, but I really needed your help." Leah looked at her sisters nervously. She wasn't sure what they were going to say. Hailey was the first one to speak.

"We get it, Leah. Though you shouldn't have treated us like that. If you had told us you wanted to learn to do it by yourself, we could've helped you. Instead, you just made us angry and upset because we wanted to work on this together."

"I know, and I'm really sorry. I promise I will try to do better. If you want, I really need your help to finish."

Hannah and Hailey looked at each other before telling Leah to come in for a hug. The three sisters hugged and forgave each other before going inside to finish the cupcakes.

It took a while to clean up the mess Leah made, but they got it done and the cupcakes were delicious. Hailey and Hannah forgave Leah, and they worked together to make the best cupcakes for their Mom.

The next week, they made the cupcakes again, and everyone loved them. Their whole family was at their house for their mother's birthday, so the girls had made quite a lot of cupcakes.

"The best thing about these cupcakes," their mom began, "Is that they were made with love by all three of my girls. I love you all so much. Thank you!"

Hailey, Hannah, and Leah all smiled at each other before taking another bite of the delicious double-chocolate cupcake with chocolate frosting.

Your family and your friends are your best gift

Christmas Wish List

Christmastime in the North Pole was always the busiest season of the year. For the Northern Elves, it was the only time of year they got to be the star of the show. Avery had finally finished the toy that she had been working on. It was a dollhouse for a little girl who lived in a small home with some other children who didn't have parents. The girl had been in the home for a long time, so Christmas was always made extra special for her.

Every year, Avery would make sure that she got this little girl's Christmas list. Her name was Bella. She remembered the first time she got Bella's list; there had only been one wish: to have a mom and dad like other children. Avery felt her little elf heart cry because she hadn't seen her own parents since she was a baby, either. But luckily for Avery, she always had family around to help her. Unlike Bella.

That first year, with Bella's wish in hand, Avery spoke to Santa Claus. *How am I supposed to make this wish come true?* she thought to herself. After speaking to Santa about it, Avery quickly realized that as much as they were magical elves, there were some things that they just couldn't do. Her heart hurt even more after that, and Avery spent her festive season checking on small Bella. That was what she was doing at this particular moment when she heard her name.

"Avery." She turned to see Santa walking up to her, eating freshly baked snickerdoodle cookies. He stopped beside her and stared at the screen that showed Bella reading a book.

"Hello, Santa." Avery had to talk louder than usual because she was so small compared to him.

"How's Bella doing?"

"I suppose she's okay. I got her Christmas list here," Avery said and showed the list to Santa.

"She asked for parents again." Santa replied as he read the few wishes on her list.

"She asks for them every year. At least she's adding some more wishes this time so we can make those come true."

Santa nodded his head as he passed the note back to Avery. They both stared at Bella in silence for a while before Santa said something else.

"Maybe this year we could try to make all her wishes come true."

"What do you mean, Santa?" Instead of answering her straight away, Santa smiled and asked Avery to follow him.

***

"Bella?" The little girl looked up at Ms. Charlotte as she walked into the room. She had been reading "Rudolph The Red-Nosed Reindeer," her favorite Christmas story because it reminded Bella of her parents.

"Yes, Ms. Charlotte?" At seven years old and having been in the home for three years, she knew the different looks of her caretaker. Some days she looked really sad or angry, but today she had a smile on her face which had Bella wondering what was happening.

"There's some people I would like you to meet. Is that okay?" Ms. Charlotte asked, and Bella didn't know what to say. For as long as she's been there, no one has asked to see her. Bella stared at Ms. Charlotte with scared eyes.

"Bella, it's okay if you're scared or shy. They are very nice people, I promise you. They are actually some of my best friends and they would love to meet you."

Still a bit scared, Bella grabbed her hand and the two of them walked to the meeting area together. When Bella saw the two people sitting at the table, she was surprised that they looked a lot like her birth parents. Sitting down, Ms. Charlotte introduced her friends as Kelly and Todd Stanton. They had friendly smiles on their faces which made her feel better about being there with them.

Bella greeted Kelly and Todd with a small smile of her own. As time went on and they all talked, Bella became less shy and started feeling excited. She was enjoying herself and laughing like she hadn't done in a while.

"So, what did you ask Santa for this year?" Mrs. Stanton asked after they had finished laughing at Mr. Stanton's joke. Bella said nothing for a bit, as she knew what she asked for wouldn't come true.

"I asked for a dollhouse, some reading books, and this teddy bear that I used to have before I came here," she whispered,

playing with her hands in her lap.

"Can you tell us about your bear, please?" Mr. Stanton asked.

"It was a Winnie The Pooh bear. He was yellow and wore a red shirt. Pooh Bear was my favorite toy, but I lost him." Bella had tears in her eyes when she spoke about the bear. He was the last gift her parents gave her and she missed him very much.

For the rest of the afternoon, Bella spent time getting to know the Stanton's. They seemed very interested in her and made sure she always felt comfortable and safe. When they left, Bella went back to her room and played with some toys for a while. There was a knock on her door and Ms. Charlotte asked to come in.

"What did you think of Mr. and Mrs. Stanton?" Ms. Charlotte asked as she sat down on the floor with Bella.

"I like them. They were very nice and funny."

Ms. Charlotte smiled at her answer and said, "They really like you as well. They asked if you would be okay if they came back tomorrow and spent more time with you. Would that be okay, Bella?"

"Sure! I like them," she said excitedly.

The next day, the Stanton's came to the home early in the morning and spent the whole day with Bella. They had a picnic for lunch and played around the garden in the warm sunshine. Bella really liked Kelly and Todd and began to love spending time with them. For the next few weeks, they spent a lot of time together. They even got special permission from Ms. Charlotte to leave the home for some outings. Of course, Ms. Charlotte had to come along so someone else looked after the other children. But Bella didn't mind because she was having a lot of fun.

She felt sad that her actual parents weren't with her, but the Stanton's were quickly becoming very important to Bella as well.

It was now Christmas Eve and the children in the home were gathered around the Christmas tree, eating cookies and reading stories. It was just about to be Bella's turn to read when Ms. Charlotte came in with Mr. and Mrs. Stanton. She immediately smiled when she saw them and ran to give them tight hugs.

"Mr. and Mrs. Stanton! What are you doing here?" Bella asked excitedly, and the two adults smiled at her.

"Well, we were hoping we could talk to you for a moment, if you don't mind?" Mr. Stanton asked. Bella looked at her caretaker and Ms. Charlotte nodded her head with a smile as well.

They followed Ms. Charlotte into the dining hall, where they had some privacy.

"Bella, we wanted to give you a Christmas present." Mrs. Stanton gave her a gift bag and when she opened it, Bella started to cry. It was a Winnie The Pooh bear.

She gave them both big hugs and thanked them for the special gift. She felt very happy to have Pooh Bear again.

"That's not all though." Bella looked at the two of them

quizzically, wondering what else they wanted.

"Bella, Todd and I would like to adopt you. Only if you want us to," Mrs. Stanton said gently.

"You want to adopt me? Why?" She looked at them in surprise.

Mrs. Stanton bent down to look Bella in the eyes, and Mr. Stanton followed. "You are a very special girl, Bella. Over the time we have spent together, we felt a strong connection with you. We love you and want you to be a part of our family."

"Kelly is right, Bella. We love you. What do you say?"

Bella stared at the nervous faces of the two people who wanted to be her parents. Slowly, she nodded her head yes, and they hugged each other as a family. She was now Bella Stanton, daughter of Todd and Kelly.

***

"You see, Avery. Sometimes we can't make all their wishes come true. But that doesn't mean that we can't guide someone else's wish in the right direction," Santa said to the little elf as they both watched the screen. The Stanton's had just adopted Bella and Avery couldn't be happier.

"You're right, Santa. I guess we really did make all her Christmas wishes come true." Avery turned to high-five Santa. Both Avery the Elf and Santa Claus looked at the happy family with joy in their eyes. Another Christmas wish had come true.

Thank you for buying our book!

If you find this storybook fun and useful, we would be very grateful if you could post a short review on Amazon! Your support does make a difference and we read every review personally.

If you would like to leave a review, just head on over to this book's Amazon page and click "Write a customer review."

Thank you for your support!

Printed in Great Britain
by Amazon